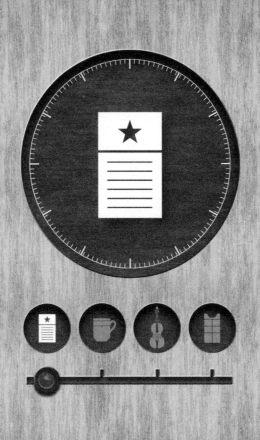

by STEVE BREZENOFF

RETURN TO
TITANIC

TIME VOYAGE

1

ILLUSTRATED by SCOTT MURPHY

STONE ARCH BOOKS A CAPSTONE IMPRINT

WHITE STAR LINE

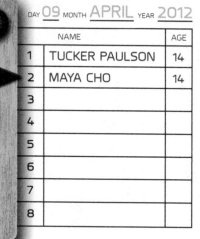

★ SHIP **R.M.S. TITANIC** WEIGHT **46,000** [TONS]

DAY 09 MONTH APRIL YEAR 2012

	NAME	AGE
1	TUCKER PAULSON	14
2	MAYA CHO	14
3		
4		
5		
6		
7		
8		

Published by Stone Arch Books – A Capstone Imprint • 1710 Roe Crest Drive, North Mankato, Minnesota 56003
www.capstonepub.com

Library of Congress Cataloging-in-Publication Data is available on the Library of Congress website.
Library binding: 978-1-4342-3299-1 • Paperback: 978-1-4342-3909-9

Summary: When Tucker and Maya are sent back in time to *Titanic*'s maiden voyage, they must save a new
friend before it's too late.

Image Credits: Newscom: UPI Photo Service/Ezio Petersen, 110; Premier Exhibitions RMS Titanic, Inc./©Bill
Sauder Collection, 111

Editor: Alison Deering
Designer and Art Director: Bob Lentz
Creative Director: Heather Kindseth

Printed in the United States of America in Stevens Point, Wisconsin.
102012 006960R

CONTENTS

NEW YORK

GREENVILLE

★ WHITE STAR LINE
04.09.2012

1

SPRING BREAK

"It's a plate," Tucker Paulsen said. He wasn't impressed. The thing his mother was holding up was just a plate — a fancy one, and sort of small, but still . . . just a plate.

Tucker was sitting on a bench in the front hall of the Greenville History Museum. Next to him was his best friend, Maya Cho. Tucker and Maya were in the same eighth-grade class at Greenville Junior High. It was the first Monday morning of their spring vacation. Maya's parents both had to work, so her dad had dropped her off at the museum that morning to spend the day with Tucker.

Maya leaned forward and squinted at the plate. "Yup," she said. "It's definitely a plate."

The museum wasn't open yet, but Tucker's mother was the curator. During vacation, Tucker and Maya would be spending every day, from eight in the morning 'til five in the afternoon, at the museum.

This is some vacation, Tucker thought, rolling his eyes. He tugged his baseball hat tighter onto his head. He hated when he got stuck helping his mom at work. Sitting around in a dusty museum looking at dishes was so boring. *I still don't understand why I can't just stay home alone*, he thought.

Tucker's mother held up

the plate, smiling and showing it off like a model on a game show.

Maya covered her mouth to stop a giggle. "It really is just a plate, Mrs. Paulsen," she said. "What's the big deal?"

"Seriously, Mom," Tucker said. He pulled a comic book from his back pocket and flipped it open. "Big whoop."

"Actually, it's a tea saucer," Tucker's mom told them as she carefully put the little plate back in its case. "And it is a very big whoop. It is a huge whoop."

Tucker and Maya looked at each other and rolled their eyes.

"This plate," Mom went on, "and everything else that arrived for this new exhibit, are all from the *Titanic*."

"The movie?" Maya said. Her face lit up with excitement. "I love that movie," she went on. "It's so romantic. Jack and Rose are like the best couple ever."

Tucker pretended to puke. Then he pulled his baseball hat even tighter onto his head.

"Not from the movie, Maya," Mom replied. "All these artifacts are from the actual boat! This year marks the hundredth anniversary of its maiden — and only — voyage."

Tucker sighed and turned to Maya. "Sorry you're stuck with me at the museum this week, Maya," he whispered. "It's officially the most boring place in town."

Maya shrugged. "Beats the alternative. I'd rather come to work here with your mom than go to my dad's stuffy office," she said. "And I have no interest in helping my mom clean houses all week, believe me."

"You might change your mind," Tucker replied. "Cleaning houses will probably look great after a week here."

"That's enough out of you, Tucker," Mom said. "I'm sure Maya will have a great week at the museum with us. She'll learn a lot."

"See?" Tucker whispered. "What did I tell you? Boring."

If Tucker's mom heard his comment, she ignored it. "This isn't going to be all fun and games," she went on. "I'm counting on a little help from you two this week, since you don't have anything better to do."

Tucker held up his comic. "I have this comic," he said. "It's way better."

Maya laughed. Mom scowled. "Tucker," Mom said. She snatched the comic away and held it behind her back. "You should be especially interested in helping."

"Why is that?" Tucker asked. He tried to grab the comic back, but Mom dodged him.

"Because your great-great-grandfather was a passenger onboard the *Titanic*," she said. "That's why."

"He was?" Tucker asked.

Maya tossed her short, straight black hair. "Wait a minute," she said. "Didn't the *Titanic* sink?"

"Of course," Mrs. Paulsen said.

"Then how could Tucker's great-great-great-grandfather have been onboard?" Maya asked. Her forehead wrinkled in confusion. "Wouldn't he have, you know . . ."

"Died?" Tucker finished. He made another grab for his comic, but his mom dodged out of the way.

"That's one too many 'greats,' Maya," Mom said. "Besides, not everyone onboard the *Titanic* died when it sank, as you know if you've watched the movie. Some people got to a lifeboat in time and were rescued."

"Huh," Maya said. She shrugged. "I guess I was too busy watching Leonardo DiCaprio to notice."

"Tucker's great-great-grandfather was especially lucky," Mom added. "He was a third-class passenger and still survived. Most third-class passengers onboard the *Titanic* died. He lost both his parents in the wreck."

"That's awful," Maya said. "He must have been so scared."

"I'll say," Tucker's mom said. She put an arm around Tucker. "He arrived in New York as an orphan. His aunt raised him after that. A woman named Moira, I believe."

Tucker's mom handed him his comic back, but she gave him a look. Tucker knew what that look meant: time to help.

He groaned, but put away his comic. "Fine, we'll help," Tucker said. "What do you need us to do?"

"That's my little assistant curator," Mrs. Paulsen said, smiling. "Let's get started."

NEW YORK

GREENVILLE

THE ASSISTANT CURATORS

Mrs. Paulsen led Tucker and Maya into a room at the back of the museum. The room was huge. It was lined with rows upon rows of shelves, all full of crates and bottles and cases and sacks.

Tucker wrinkled his nose as they entered the storage room. "I'll never get used to the smell," he said.

The room smelled like an old book, but a hundred times as strong. And on top of that was the odor of rubber, like a new tire, and the smell of grease, like the floor of a garage.

"Wow," Maya said, looking around at all of the shelves. "What is all this stuff?"

"This is where we keep exhibits before a new show starts," Mrs. Paulsen said, "or when we need more room on the floor."

"On the floor?" Maya asked. As she walked through the room, she ran a finger along a low shelf covered with dust.

"That means out where everyone can see them," Tucker said. "On display."

"Oh . . ." Maya said. She nodded. "Gotcha."

"The *Titanic* crates have mostly been unpacked, but there are still a few left to look through," Mrs. Paulsen said. She led Maya and Tucker to a small crate way in the back behind some cabinets.

"This crate wasn't on the shipping manifest the museum received, so we don't know what's in it," Mrs. Paulsen said. "I need you two to go through it and make a list of everything you find so we can account for it." She handed Maya a pad of paper and a pen.

"Got it," Maya said.

"I'm going to be out on the museum floor," Mrs. Paulsen continued. "I want to make sure the exhibit is perfect for the opening later this morning."

"Okay, Mom," Tucker said, rolling his eyes. "It's just opening a box and making a list, not rocket science. I think we can handle it."

As she walked off, Mom called over her shoulder, "And be careful!"

"We will," Maya and Tucker shouted.

Once his mom was gone, Tucker looked around the room. "Let's get started, I guess," he said. He walked over and opened a tool box sitting on the ground near the crate. He pulled out a heavy screwdriver, slid it between the crate and its cover, and pried off the top.

All they could see at first was padding material: strips of newspaper and foam peanuts, right up to the rim. But lying across the top was a piece of paper that was boldly stamped with the words:

SPECIAL COLLECTION
HANDLE WITH CARE

"Ooh," Maya said. "There must be important stuff in here. Do you think we should tell your mom?"

"Nah," Tucker said. "She doesn't like me to bug her once she gives me a job. She always says she'd rather I learn to figure it out on my own. Let's just get started."

"Okay," Maya said. She uncapped her pen and opened the notebook to the first page. "So, what's in there?"

"Well, one piece of paper," Tucker said, holding up the big note.

"Besides the paper, dork," Maya said, shaking her head.

Tucker reached in and pulled out a big armful of packing material. "Okay, there's a fancy teacup," he said. "It's in a hard plastic case." He held the case up.

The cup inside the case was small and blue. It had a white band circling the top, with a gold design around it. It looked like something the queen of England might use to drink tea.

"Teacup," Maya said. She wrote it down. "Got it. What else?"

"Let's see," Tucker said. He dug through some more packing material. "There's a life vest, in a sealed, clear plastic bag." He held it up.

"Gross," Maya said.

It was gross. The life vest was a sickening brown color, and most of the fabric and stitches were torn. The straps were all cut or broken. Along the front, six pockets — three on each side of the vest — were torn or missing completely.

Tucker shrugged. "I guess it's pretty nasty," he admitted. "Still, add it to the list."

Maya scribbled it down. "It looks used," she said. "Maybe it saved someone's life."

"Could be," Tucker said. He gave the life vest another long look before setting it aside.

"Okay, what else is there?" Maya asked. She tapped her bottom lip with the back of the pen.

"A slip of paper in a plastic envelope," Tucker said. "Oh, wait." He grabbed the plastic sleeve the paper was in and took a closer look. "It's a boarding pass," he said. "A *Titanic* boarding pass."

The ticket was bigger than Tucker would have thought. It was almost the size of small paperback book. Along the top, it read, "White Star Line," and beneath that, "Royal and United States Mail Steamers." Below it listed the port of departure as Queenstown, Ireland and the date as the 11th day of April in the year 1912.

"Wow," Maya said as she wrote it down. "I can't believe there are any around still. Maybe it belonged to your great-great-great-great-grandfather!"

"That's too many 'greats' again," Tucker said. "Okay, there's one more thing in here. A smashed violin in a hard plastic case."

The violin was in bad shape. It had no strings, and the body of the instrument was cracked and covered with splintery holes. The neck of the violin was bent and only stayed connected to the body by a few thin strips of wood. It looked unbelievably fragile, like if someone touched it, it would fall apart instantly.

"Busted violin," Maya said as she wrote it down. "Got it. Is that it?"

Tucker took out all the packing material. The crate was empty.

"That's it," Tucker said.

Maya put down the pad and leaned forward. She pushed her hair behind her ear and reached for the ticket. "Let me see that," she said.

Tucker handed it to her. "Be careful," he said. "If anything happens to this stuff, my mom will freak."

"I know, I know," Maya said. She squinted at the ticket through the plastic sleeve. Then she turned the ticket over in her hands. "I just want to see if there's a name on it," she said.

"Why?" Tucker asked. He pulled out his comic book and flipped it open.

"It might be your great-great-grandfather's," Maya said.

"I seriously doubt it," Tucker said. "There were like a million tickets."

"What was his name?" Maya said.

"I have no idea," Tucker said. "I have, what, like sixteen great-great-grandfathers, right?"

Maya shrugged. "If you say so," she said. Then her eyes lit up. "Oh, here it is!"

She put the ticket right up to her face. With her thumbs, she tried to smooth out the plastic, but a seam and some tape covered the spot where the name was written on the ticket.

"I can't read it," she said. "I'm going to have to take it out of the plastic."

"What?!" Tucker said. He threw down his comic and reached for the ticket. "Don't open it!"

Maya pulled the ticket away quickly and laughed. "Why not?" she said. "I'll be careful. I can't read the name without taking it out."

Tucker grabbed for the ticket again and missed. "Then don't read the name," he said. "You'll live."

Maya jumped up and ran behind a stack of crates. She laughed as she pulled away the strip of tape that kept the plastic sleeve closed.

"Don't do that!" Tucker shouted. "My mom will kill us. She'll kill you!"

"Oh, please," Maya said. "Relax!" She slipped two fingers into the sleeve to pull out the ticket.

Tucker leaped at her and grabbed for the ticket at the same time.

For an instant, both their hands were on the ticket as it slid out of the plastic. But an instant was all it took.

3

ON THE DOCKS

Tucker could tell that something strange had happened even before he opened his eyes. Something was off.

The musky smell of the museum storage room was gone. Instead, the air hung heavily with the scents of salt and fish and garbage.

The quiet of the museum had been replaced with a variety of sounds. Boots trampled heavily across wooden planks. Voices chattered excitedly. Others shouted goodbyes to one other. The chime of church bells rang out. The noises were accompanied by the sound of waves crashing against the shore.

"Ugh . . ." Tucker said as he sat up. He was dizzy. And his head hurt. A lot. He put a hand on his head and opened his eyes. The sun was shining high in the sky, and Tucker had to squint.

"What . . ." Maya began. She was next to him, struggling to sit up. "What happened? Where are we?"

"I don't know," Tucker said. He shook his head, and the pain began to fade. His eyes adjusted to the bright sunlight, and he looked around.

He and Maya were still surrounded by wooden crates, but these boxes were very different from the ones at the museum. They looked much older and more weathered. Some were stamped with the words, "White Star Line." Canvas mailbags were scattered among the crates.

We're definitely not in the museum anymore, Tucker realized. He shook his head again and tried to focus on his surroundings. He looked down at the wooden planks beneath him. They were on a dock. The water couldn't be that far away, Tucker figured, because he could clearly hear the splash of waves against the pier.

In front of them, where the wooden dock met the streets, sat a low, wide building. It looked like it had once been painted gray. But the color had been weathered and faded by the sea air. The side of the building read "Queenstown Harbor Fishery." Beyond the building was a village with narrow brick streets.

Tucker and Maya barely had time to notice any of that, though. Beyond the crates, they could see hundreds of people in old-fashioned clothing standing on the docks. Most of the people were carrying luggage. They were all rushing and shouting to one another. Kids of all ages laughed and ran across the dock. Anxious mothers tried to grab them. Fathers only laughed and smoked their pipes.

Just then a bell clanged loudly at the end of the pier and startled Tucker out of his stupor. He elbowed Maya and pointed at the water. Two small boats were pulling in.

"Where are we?" Maya asked again. She rubbed the back of her head.

Tucker shook his head. "I have no idea," he said, "but I don't think we're in Greenville anymore."

Maya tapped him on the shoulder. "Look!" she said. When Tucker turned, he saw she was pointing to a sign on the building behind them.

"What does that mean?" Tucker asked.

Maya shrugged. "You got me," she said.

Tucker felt something in his hand. He looked down to find himself clutching a crumpled piece of paper. He opened it up. It was the *Titanic* ticket from his mother's museum, and right along the top it read "White Star Line."

"Wow," Tucker whispered.

"What?" Maya said.

"The White Star Line is the company that sailed the *Titanic*!" Tucker said.

"What's your point?" Maya asked.

"Look around us! Everyone is dressed so old-fashioned," Tucker said. "And they're all crowding around, like they're in some kind of big hurry."

"So?" Maya said, rolling her eyes. "What's your point?"

"My point is that the box was marked 'Special Collection, Handle With Care,'" Tucker said. "And I think I know why. Because if you touch that ticket, it sends you back in time."

"No way," Maya said. She shook her head. "That's not possible. You think we touched the ticket, and it sent us back to its own time?"

Tucker nodded. "What else could it be?" he asked. "Do you have another explanation?" He looked at the ticket. His mouth hung open in awe. "Mom always says there's magic in the junk at the museum," he said, "but I never thought she meant for real!"

Maya crossed her arms over her chest. "Do you seriously think one of those things is the *Titanic*?" she said, pointing at the boats that were docking. They looked like modern-day tugboats. Each one was filled with passengers ready to disembark.

Tucker shrugged. "Maybe," he said. "How should I know?"

"Those are way too small," Maya said. "The *Titanic* was the largest passenger boat in the world when it sank."

"How do you know so much about it?" Tucker asked. "Just because you saw the movie doesn't mean you're an expert."

"Well, I obviously know more than you do!" Maya protested.

Just then, a shadow fell over Maya and Tucker. They turned around. A boy their own age was standing over them. He was wearing a dark-colored suit and a funny cap.

"The *Titanic* sank?" the boy repeated. "The *Titanic* hasn't even left Queenstown yet. What do you mean, it sank?"

QUEENSTOWN

LONDON

SOUTHAMPTON

★ WHITE STAR LINE
04.11.1912

THIRD-CLASS TICKETS

4

"You shouldn't sneak up on people like that!" Maya shrieked. She jumped to her feet and scowled at the boy. "You scared me half to death! How long have you been standing there?"

The boy raised his eyebrows at her. "I didn't sneak up on anyone," he said. He had a thick Irish accent. "I just walked normally. And I was here long enough to hear you two say some crazy things."

Maya and Tucker exchanged a quick glance. Tucker stood up. "Well, what do you want?" he asked. "We're, um, busy."

"You do not look busy," the boy said. "I don't

want anything, anyway. Da gave me a penny for the sweet shop. I was just walking past and saw you two. You look rather . . . odd."

The boy looked Maya and Tucker up and down. They did the same to him.

Of course we look odd to him, Tucker realized. *He's probably never seen anyone in jeans and T-shirts before.*

"Are you Americans, then?" the boy asked.

"Oh, yes! That's right. Americans," Maya said quickly. She nodded furiously. "We sure are."

Tucker scratched his head. "Maya, we *are* Americans," he said quietly. "Stop acting weird."

"Just leave us alone," Maya said to the boy. "Mind your own business."

"All right," the boy said. "I have to hurry and get on the ship, anyhow."

"The *Titanic*?" Tucker asked. "Are you getting on the *Titanic*?"

"Of course," the boy said. "My family is emigrating to America. Aren't you getting on as

well? I assumed the both of you were going back to America."

"Get on the *Titanic*?" Maya said. "What are you, crazy?"

The boy gave Maya a long look. "I'm not sure I like you," the boy said.

"She takes some getting used to," Tucker said, smiling. "Anyway, which of those two boats is the *Titanic*?"

The boy looked over at the boats, then at Tucker, then back at the boats. Then he started to laugh.

"Those two boats?" he repeated, still laughing. "Neither of those is the *Titanic*. Are you daft? The *Titanic* doesn't even fit in the Queenstown Harbor."

"Told you so," Maya muttered under her breath.

Tucker ignored her. He turned to the boy. "But you said . . ." Tucker began.

"Those are the tenders," the boy explained.

"They'll be carrying the passengers out to the *Titanic*."

"That's impossible," Maya said. "I know I've seen photographs of the *Titanic* at the dock. That's how people got on!"

The boy took a step back. "They might have boarded from the docks in Southampton," he said.

"England?" Tucker asked.

"Of course," the boy said. "That's where most of the passengers boarded. People there might have boarded right from the dock, up the gangplank. But I don't see how you would have seen a photograph of that already. It only happened yesterday."

Maya started to respond, but Tucker covered her mouth quickly. "Ignore her," he said. "She's — what was the word you used? — daft!"

The boy nodded, but he looked suspicious.

Tucker looked down. He still held the ticket from the museum in his hand. "Can I see your ticket?" he asked.

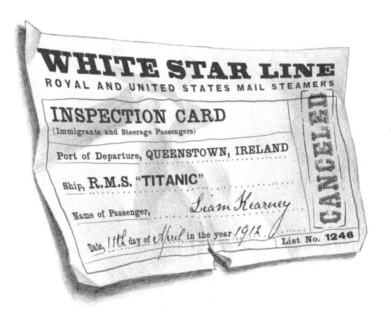

"I thought you weren't sailing today," the boy said. He held out his own ticket.

"Um, right. Maya's not getting on," Tucker said. He reached out and took the other boy's ticket. "But I have a ticket."

Tucker compared the two tickets. They were identical. They were both third-class tickets, sold by the same travel agency, for boarding the *Titanic* at Queenstown on April 11, 1912. Even the passenger's name was the same: Liam Kearney.

WHITE STAR LINE
ROYAL AND UNITED STATES MAIL STEAMERS

INSPECTION CARD
(Immigrants and Steerage Passengers)

Port of Departure, **QUEENSTOWN, IRELAND**

Ship, **R.M.S. "TITANIC"**

Name of Passenger, *Liam Kearney*

Date, *11th* day of *April* in the year *1912*

List No. **1246**

Tucker's eyes widened as he realized what that meant. The ticket Tucker's mom had in her collection — which Tucker now held in his hand — was this boy's ticket. The only difference was that Tucker's version had already been stamped canceled, since it had already been used. A hundred years ago.

Tucker quickly pulled his ticket away before Liam could see his own name on someone else's ticket.

"Liam!" a woman shouted. The three kids looked up and saw a woman waving from the line to board the tenders. A man was standing next to her. "Liam," she shouted again, "hurry up now, Liam!"

"That's my mum," Liam said. "I guess I missed my chance to get a chocolate. I'd better go." He waved as he walked off toward his parents.

Tucker waved goodbye as the Irish boy moved away. Then he remembered what his mom had said back at the museum. If this boy and his parents were boarding the *Titanic* as third-class passengers, they probably wouldn't survive.

SAVING THE KEARNEYS

"Maya, we have to stop him," Tucker said, watching Liam walk back to his parents. "He's a third-class passenger. If he gets on the *Titanic*, he could die when the ship sinks."

"So?" Maya said.

"What do you mean, 'so'?" Tucker said. "We can't just let him and his family drown."

"Tucker, don't you get it?" Maya asked. "Liam and his parents might die, true. But if they're meant to, then they already have. There's nothing we can do about it."

"Um," Tucker said. "They're right there, waiting in line. They haven't drowned."

"I mean, in our time," Maya said. "You know, back in the twenty-first century, where we're supposed to be?"

"So we're supposed to just let him die?" Tucker asked.

"What's the alternative? Messing with events that have already happened? I don't think that's a great idea either," Maya said. She squinted at the display on her cell phone. "Ugh. No service."

Tucker closed his eyes and shook his head. "Of course there's no service," he said. "How could there be service?"

"What? We're in Ireland," Maya said. "People in Ireland use cell phones."

Tucker just stared at her.

"Don't they?" Maya asked. She tapped her phone again, then sighed and slipped it into her bag.

"Okay," Tucker said. "Tell you what. You sit here and wait for someone to launch a cell phone satellite. I'm going to try to convince Liam and his parents to stay off that boat!"

Maya sighed. "Fine, fine," she grumbled. "I'll help. Sheesh. But could you not forget the bigger issue here? We need to figure out how we're going to get back to the present!"

Tucker nodded once. "I know," he said with a sigh. "It's not exactly something that's easy to forget. We'll work on both problems at the same time, okay?"

Tucker ran over to the long line of passengers and spotted Liam quickly. He was standing with a woman who wore a long, drab dress. Tucker immediately liked her face. There was something familiar about her, but he wasn't quite sure what it was.

Next to the woman stood a tall man with a mustache. He was smoking a pipe and had a newspaper folded under his arm. Tucker figured that had to be Liam's father.

"Wait, Liam," Tucker said when he caught up to the small family. "You can't get on that boat!"

"Of course we can," Liam's father said. "We

have tickets." He looked at his son and said, "Liam, do you know this boy?"

"Yes, Da," Liam said. "And that girl," he added, nodding toward Maya as she walked up. "I met them earlier, when I was looking for the sweet shop."

"Hi," Maya said. "Ignore my friend here. He's, um, daft."

Maya quickly took Tucker by the arm and started dragging him away.

"Wait," Tucker said as she pulled him away. "Don't get on that boat!" he called to Liam's family.

As Maya dragged him away, Tucker heard Liam's father saying, "Those children were so odd. Did you see those strange clothes they were wearing? They must be Americans . . . I certainly hope everyone there isn't so odd."

Maya pulled Tucker around the corner of the dock building. "Will you please shut up?" she demanded.

"Me?" Tucker said in disbelief. "I'm trying to save them."

"And what exactly are you planning to tell them?" Maya asked. "That you're from the future? That you came back in time by touching their son's magic ticket and have to warn them that the most famous ocean liner ever is going to sink?! Everyone will think you're crazy!"

"I have to do something!" Tucker said. He looked at his feet.

"They'll lock you up," Maya told him. "They'll put us both in the loony bin and throw away the key. Then we'll never figure out how to get back."

"So what exactly do you suggest?" Tucker asked.

"I'd suggest we figure out how to get home," Maya said, "and stop trying to change history. The ticket has to be the key to getting back. Let me see it."

Maya reached forward to grab the magical ticket out of Tucker's hand. But just before she

touched it, they heard a commotion underneath the dock.

Maya put a finger to her lips. Then she got down on her knees and squinted between the dock planks. She waved her hand and motioned for Tucker to join her.

Underneath the dock, Tucker saw, there was a man. He was wearing a hat pulled low over his face and crawling along the rocks with a heavy-looking satchel on his back.

"What do you think he's doing?" Maya asked. "Trying to sneak onto a ship?"

Tucker shook his head. "The boats are in the other direction," he said.

Then, suddenly, the man was out of sight. He disappeared between planks.

"Where'd he go?" Maya asked. She peered between the planks again. "He's gone."

"I don't know. I can't see him anymore," Tucker said. "He must have come to shore or gone underwater."

"Come to shore it is," said a voice behind them.

The two kids spun, and there was the man from under the dock. He dropped his bag, and it landed with a thud. Then he reached out to grab them.

6

JOHN COFFEY

"Let go of us!" Maya shouted.

The man held her and Tucker tightly by their shirt collars. "Why were you little scraps spying on me, then?" he demanded in a thick Irish brogue. He snarled and bared his teeth like a wild animal. His eyes narrowed with anger as he glared at them. He was dressed in a dark suit. The jacket was open, and its silver buttons caught the sunlight.

"We weren't spying!" Tucker said. He tried desperately to pull away, but the man was unbelievably strong.

"Don't try to lie to me," the man growled.

"It's true!" Maya said. "We just heard something under the dock, and we were trying to see what it was. We're not interested in your business!"

The man glared at them for a moment longer, then let go of their shirts. They landed on the hard planks of the dock.

"Ow," Maya said. "So . . . what were you doing under the dock, anyway?"

The man picked up his bag and started to walk off. "You two had best mind your own affairs," he said as he left.

"Please wait!" Tucker said. He and Maya got to their feet and ran after the man.

"Are you a crewman on the *Titanic*?" Maya asked.

Without stopping or turning around, the man said, "Not anymore, lassie."

"But you used to be?" Tucker asked.

"Did you desert the ship?" Maya asked breathlessly.

The man finally stopped and turned to face them. Tucker and Maya had to skid to a stop to avoid running into him. He leaned down, close to their faces, and Tucker could smell the tobacco on his breath.

"Listen here, the two of you," he said. "My name is Coffey. John Coffey. And I was a fireman on the *Titanic* long enough. From Southampton to France to Queenstown. I plan to skip the trip to New York. You two would be wise to do the same."

He stood up straight and looked around. The view seemed to cheer him up.

"I'm home now," the man went on. "My mum is in Queenstown. I was born here, and I aim to stay here. If you have a lick of sense in you, you'll stay put as well."

He leaned down again and stared hard at the two kids. "Have you got tickets?" he asked.

Tucker held out the magical ticket, and the man glanced at it. "Rip it up," the man said.

"Don't!" Maya said quickly, reaching out her hand to stop Tucker. She leaned closer and whispered, "We need that to get back home, remember?"

Tucker shushed her. "I know," he whispered back. Then he turned back to John Coffey.

"Why should I?" Tucker asked.

"As sure as we're standing here now," the man said, "*Titanic* will sink. Mark my words."

7

PROGNOSTICATOR

"How do you know?" Maya asked. "Why do you think the *Titanic* will sink?"

"I'm a Coffey," the man said. "My family has always had special dreams. When we sleep at night, we don't just dream. We see the future. We're what they call prognosticators. Well, last night I had a dream."

"About the ship?" Tucker asked.

Coffey nodded. "Aye," he said. "I dreamed I was in my cabin onboard. Suddenly it was filling with seawater. I couldn't breathe or reach the surface. I was drowning."

"Maybe you're just scared," Maya suggested.

Coffey looked angry again. He opened his mouth to reply, but just before he spoke, Liam Kearney walked up to them.

"If you two are going to get on one of the tenders, you'd better come back to the line," Liam said. "They're beginning to board."

Coffey shook his head. "Best of luck to you three," he said.

"Wait!" Tucker said. He grabbed Coffey's sleeve. The man looked down at Tucker's hand and snarled.

"Please, come convince Liam's family not to board, at least," Tucker said.

Coffey looked over at the line, where Liam's mother was waving frantically to her son. Then Coffey looked at Liam.

"Are you a Kearney?" Coffey asked.

Liam nodded.

"Then your da is Patrick Kearney?" Coffey asked.

Liam nodded again. "Yes, sir," he said.

Coffey turned to Tucker. "Sorry," he said. "The Kearneys and Coffeys in Queenstown have never trusted each other. The boy's da thinks our dreams are bunk, and I don't blame him for that. It would stretch any man's faith to believe a clairvoyant like myself. But the fact remains, he won't listen to me. You're on your own. Best of luck to you."

Coffey waved and tossed his bag over his shoulder. Then he walked around the dock house and down a narrow lane into the city itself, leaving Tucker, Maya, and Liam staring after him.

20°

0°

20°

LONDON

QUEENSTOWN

SOUTHAMPTON

★ WHITE STAR LINE
04.11.1912

LEAVE WITHOUT US

Across the dock, a porter called out, "All aboard the *America*!"

"That's the tender," Liam said. He grabbed Maya and Tucker and added, "We have to go now, or they'll leave without us!" He started pulling them toward the line.

"Let them," Maya muttered. "We have to get home, Tucker!" But both boys ignored her. Maya sighed loudly. Reluctantly, she followed Liam and Tucker back to where Liam's parents stood waiting.

"Please listen to me," Tucker said when they reached the Kearneys. "You can't get on that boat."

Liam's mother put her arms around her son. "What on earth are you talking about?" she asked, looking annoyed. "Why not?"

Mr. Kearney chuckled. "I spent three months' pay on these tickets," he said. "We're done in Ireland. We've already packed up all our things. We've said our goodbyes. Besides, my sister is in New York waiting for us. She's never even met Liam, because she's been gone so long. We can't just turn back now."

Mr. Kearney turned away, clearly signaling that the discussion was finished.

Tucker looked at his feet. *There's no way I'll be able to convince these people*, he thought. *Maya's right. They'll think I'm crazy.*

"Maybe you're right, Maya," Tucker said quietly as the line edged forward toward the tender. "Maybe we have no choice. Let's just figure out how to get back to our own time."

Maya sighed. She was relieved that Tucker was finally talking seriously about getting home, instead of worrying about this family they didn't even know. Still, the thought of their new friend and his parents boarding the doomed ship made her sad. She knew they would likely never live to see New York.

Then she snapped her fingers and her face brightened. "I have an idea," she said.

"What?" Tucker asked.

"Just follow my lead," Maya said.

Tucker frowned. "Okay," he said.

"Hey, Mr. Kearney," Maya said. "Do you miss your sister?"

"Of course," Liam's father replied. "I haven't seen her in years."

"If you get on the *Titanic*, you'll probably never see her again," Maya said.

"What's this?" Mr. Kearney asked. "What are you talking about, lass?"

"Tell him, Tucker," Maya said.

"Me?" Tucker asked. "Why me?"

Maya frowned. "It was your idea," she said.

Tucker blinked at her. "What was?" he whispered.

"To tell them the truth," Maya said urgently through her teeth.

"Fine," Tucker said. He took a deep breath and went on. "Sir, the *Titanic* is going to sink in the middle of the Atlantic. There are nowhere near enough lifeboats for everyone on board. A lot of people are going to die. Most of the third-class passengers will never reach America."

Liam's mother gasped. She hugged her son tighter with one arm and put her other hand over her mouth. Liam's father's jaw dropped, and he nearly lost his pipe.

"That's ridiculous," Mr. Kearney said. "Where would you get such an idea?"

"Ridiculous indeed," Mrs. Kearney said. "Why, I read in the paper last week that the *Titanic* is the best ship man has ever built. It's the biggest passenger ship in the world. From stern to bow, everything is top of the line and the latest technology."

TITANIC SAILS!
LARGEST VESSEL IN WORLD IS "BEST MAN HAS EVER BUILT"

LONDON, 9 April–The White Star liner *Titanic* will sail at noon tomorrow from Southampton en route to New York.

The biggest passenger ship in the world, *Titanic* is an improvement over her sister ship, *Olympic*. From stern to bow, its design and construction is top of the line, using all of today's newest technology.

Capt. Smith will take

Mr. Kearney nodded as his wife spoke. "That's right," he said. "*Titanic* is a perfectly-engineered vessel. Nothing to fear. She's unsinkable, I'm told. It's the only way to cross."

Tucker and Maya exchanged a quick glance. Then they both spoke at once.

"John Coffey told us," Maya said.

"We're from the future," Tucker said.

They both grimaced. Neither of them was helping their story.

Mr. Kearney laughed. "You two had better get your stories straight," he said. "But if you've been speaking to that ruffian Coffey, I'll end our conversation now."

"Yeah," Maya said, "he said you'd say that."

"Then for once he was right," Mr. Kearney said. "Now, run along. We're boarding the tender." Tucker looked up. They'd reached the front of the line.

"Please, sir," Tucker began. "If you'll just listen to —"

"That's enough," Mr. Kearney snapped. He pulled out his watch and checked the time. "Late," he muttered. He scowled at Maya and Tucker. "I don't know who you two frauds think you are. Or what your scam is. But you'd best run along before I call the authorities."

Maya and Tucker exchanged nervous glances. They quickly stepped aside. As Liam and his parents shuffled forward and walked onto the tender, Mr. Kearney shook his head. "Ridiculous children," he muttered to his wife. "How do they raise them in America?"

TO THE SHIP

9

"Final call for boarding," a voice from the tender called. "Board now for passage to *Titanic*."

The crush of passengers pushing forward to board the tender surrounded Tucker and Maya. Mothers anxiously clutched their children's hands as they pulled them forward.

Most of the people boarding the *America* appeared to be third-class passengers. Their clothing looked clean but well-worn. Most of the boys and men wore old-fashioned hats and dark suits. Many of the women wore shawls around their shoulders to guard against the cool air.

Maya pulled Tucker off to the side.

"What do we do now?" Maya asked. "They're obviously not going to listen to us. I mean, I wouldn't exactly believe us either. It sounds pretty crazy."

She and Tucker watched helplessly as the line moved forward and the Kearneys boarded the tender.

Tucker sighed and shook his head. "I don't know. Maybe you were right. Maybe it's time to give up on helping Liam and figure out how to get home," he said.

Maya gave the tenders a long look. Everyone pushed forward, trying crowd on the tender's small deck. They all chattered excitedly about the upcoming voyage. It seemed no one could wait to board the *Titanic*.

"Let's get on the tender," Maya said abruptly. She had to raise her voice to be heard above the din of the other passengers. She suddenly stepped back into line and started to climb aboard the tender.

"Now who's daft?" Tucker asked, following her. "Mr. Kearney is going to have us arrested if we don't leave them alone. Being in jail is going to make it pretty hard to get back home. And if we get on, we'll drown, too. How is that going to help anyone?" He shook his head. "Besides, haven't you been trying to get us home?"

"We can keep working on that," Maya said. "But we only have the trip out to the *Titanic* to convince Liam and his parents not to board." She took Tucker's hand and pulled him onto the tender. Maya tried to sound confident, but privately she was getting worried. What if they were stuck there forever?

By the time Maya and Tucker made it onboard, the tender was already crowded with people lining the railings to wave goodbye. Some passengers stood on the upper deck, shouting goodbyes to people on shore. People jostled for a spot along the railing to catch a last glimpse of Ireland.

"Look, I'm still worried about getting home, too," Maya said. "We still haven't figured out how to do that — or if we even can. But we're stuck here for the time being. We might as well try to help. We can just ride the tender back to the docks after everyone else is onboard."

Tucker smiled. "Thanks," he mumbled.

"But this is the last shot," Maya said. "I mean it, Tucker. The past is history. After this we have to figure out how to get ourselves home."

Maya sat down next to him on a long bench with the other passengers. "Give me that ticket," she said. "Maybe there's a clue on how to break this spell, or whatever it is."

Tucker handed it to her. When Maya turned back around, she saw Mr. Kearney on her other side.

"You two again," Mr. Kearney said.

Liam leaned forward from between his parents and waved at Maya and Tucker. "You two decided to board after all?" he asked.

"Looks that way," Maya said.

"Just to convince you three not to get onboard the *Titanic*," Tucker said. "We're trying to save you."

Liam swallowed. He was starting to look really nervous.

"Please," Mrs. Kearney said. "Haven't you scared my son enough?"

"I'm not afraid," Liam said, but his voice trembled as he spoke.

Tucker remembered his own ticket — the magic ticket. He pulled it out of his pocket.

"I can prove we're telling the truth. Look," Tucker said quietly. He held the ticket out for Mr. Kearney to see.

"We're from the future," Tucker said.

Mr. Kearney looked at the ticket. "So what?" he said. "It's just a ticket. We have three of those. All this proves is that you bought a ticket."

"But this one is your son's!" Maya said. She pointed at the name on the ticket. "Liam Kearney," she said. "It's your son's ticket."

"I have my ticket," Liam said. He held his out. "See?"

"This is no proof of time travel," Mr. Kearney said. "Liam Kearney is a fairly common name, probably even in America." He handed the ticket back to Tucker.

"But this one is canceled," Tucker said, pointing at the ticket-taker's mark. "See? It's already been used."

Mr. Kearney squinted at him and at the ticket. "Well, you probably stole it from the ticket-taker's box, then," he said. "I'm not surprised to learn you two are little thieves."

Then he sat back and pulled his cap over his eyes. "Go pester someone else," he said.

Tucker sighed and exchanged a look with Maya. It was clear the conversation was over.

QUEENSTOWN

LONDON

SOUTHAMPTON

★ WHITE STAR LINE
04.11.1912

THE
TITANIC

The ride out to the *Titanic* lasted almost thirty minutes. The tender chugged slowly through the cold Atlantic waters. While the temperature on the dock had been warm enough, the open deck of the tender was a different story. A cool breeze whipped across the water. The other passengers pulled their coats and shawls tightly around themselves to protect against the chill.

Maya and Tucker shivered. Their light clothing didn't offer much protection against the sea breeze.

Before long, the *Titanic* came into view. Maya and Tucker both gasped as they saw the ocean liner for the first time.

It was incredible. Maya and Tucker knew it was a big ship, but pulling up next to it in their little tender was positively overwhelming. The ocean liner dwarfed the *America*.

"Wow," Maya said under her breath. "I can't believe that thing is going to sink."

Tucker's jaw dropped. "I can't believe it can even float!" he said quietly.

The *Titanic* stretched almost 900 feet long. Its rudder alone was bigger than Tucker's house. The huge hull was painted a shining black, and it seemed to stretch on forever in both directions. Tucker remembered a plaque he'd seen back at the museum: The *Titanic* was as long as three football fields and as tall as an eleven-story building.

A deep yellow stripe wrapped around the top of the ship, separating the black hull from the white at the top. Four tall smokestacks rose up from the deck like giant pillars. Against the blue-green water of the harbor, *Titanic* was strikingly huge.

As Tucker and Maya watched in awe, the tender pulled up to the *Titanic*. People were handing over their tickets and beginning to board.

"What are we going to do?" Maya asked. "We can't get on!"

Tucker shook his head. "We won't," he said. "We'll just ride back to the docks. No problem."

Just then, the crowd surged forward. Eager passengers surrounded Tucker and Maya. They were being pushed toward the ticket-taker.

Liam and his parents got shoved right to the front. Tucker did, too. He found himself right next to Liam. Both of their tickets were out.

The ticket-taker grabbed Liam's ticket. He marked it canceled.

For just an instant, Liam's ticket and Tucker's magic ticket were right next to each other. It was the first time Liam had seen the two tickets side by side.

Now, with the ticket-taker's mark on both, the tickets were exactly identical.

Liam's face went white.

But it was too late. Mr. and Mrs. Kearney handed over their tickets. Liam was being shoved onboard.

"Da!" Liam said as his parents pulled him onboard the *Titanic*. "It was true!"

"What?" Mr. Kearney said.

Tucker and Maya could barely hear them over the sound of the tender's engine and the ocean waves breaking against the *Titanic*'s huge hull.

"Those two really are from the future," Liam yelled.

"Ticket!" the ticket-taker shouted. "Tickets ready, please!"

Tucker realized he was still standing there with the magic ticket in his hand. Before he could pull it back, the ticket-taker grabbed it. He started to mark it canceled, but then noticed it already had been stamped.

"Hey, what is this?" the ticket-taker asked. "Where'd you get this ticket?"

"Um, my mother," Tucker said.

"It's already canceled," the ticket-taker said. He grabbed Tucker's collar. "Little thief!"

"Maya!" Tucker called. "Help!"

Maya reached over and grabbed Tucker by the arm. For a moment, it was like tug-of-war, but the ticket-taker gave up quickly. "Bah, there's nowhere for you two to run on here," he said. "And I've got the canceled ticket. I'll deal with you when we get back to the docks."

The ticket-taker released them suddenly, and Maya and Tucker stepped back, nearly falling.

The ticket-taker looked at the magic ticket for a moment. He held it up with both hands, looked at Tucker and Maya, and ripped it in two.

Then everything went black.

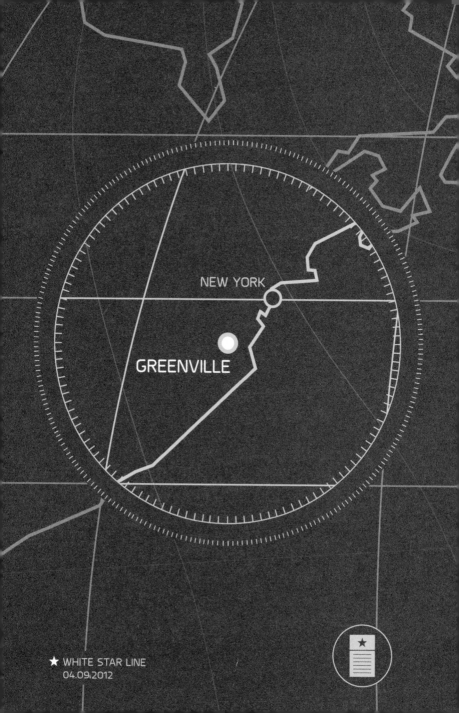

NEW YORK

GREENVILLE

HOME AGAIN

11

Someone was shaking Tucker by the shoulders. His head was pounding.

"Wake up, dork," a girl's voice said. It was Maya.

Tucker groaned.

"Come on, Tucker, wake up," she said again. "We're back."

Even before Tucker opened his eyes, he knew they were back in the storeroom at the museum. It was the smell — musty, like old books. "How did we get back?" Tucker asked.

"The ticket," Maya said. "When that ticket-taker guy ripped the ticket, it must have destroyed the magic and sent us back to our own time."

Tucker sat up. "We have to go back," he said. "Liam and his parents . . . we have to save them!"

Maya stood up. "I don't think we can," she said, shaking her head. "I think history is meant to be. You can't change it. We can't go back."

"Of course we can," Tucker said. "We just have to touch the ticket again."

"Um, the ticket is gone, remember?" Maya reminded him. "That guy ripped it up. It's probably in tiny pieces in the harbor at Queenstown. Like a hundred years ago."

"Not that ticket," Tucker said. He dug around in the Special Collection box until he felt the plastic sleeve. He pulled it out. Sure enough, the ticket was there. "See?!" he said.

"How is that possible?" Maya asked, frowning. "I saw him rip it up."

"He didn't rip the ticket Liam gave him," Tucker said. "That's the one that I have here."

Maya squinted at him. "This is making my head hurt," she said.

Tucker frantically tore off the plastic sleeve. "Ready?" he said. "We should touch it at the same time, to make sure we both go back."

"Whoa, whoa," Maya said, stepping back. "Hold on a second. What makes you think I want to go back?"

"You don't?" Tucker asked.

Maya shook her head. "I am very happy to be back home in 2012, thank you very much," she said. "Where I have full service on my phone." She held up her phone to show that it was working again. The display on the phone showed it was nearly 10 a.m., almost time for the museum to open to the public. Only an hour had passed since they'd disappeared.

Then Tucker thought of something else. "We can show Mr. Kearney your phone!" he said. "Then he'll have to believe we're from the future."

"I'm not going back!" Maya said. "Leave me out of it!"

"Please!" Tucker said. He grabbed Maya's arm.

"No way!" Maya shrieked.

"What is going on in there?" Mom called from down the hall. "Are you two all right?"

"We have to hurry," Tucker said. "My mother is coming. And we have to save Liam."

Maya glared at Tucker, but she sighed in resignation. "Fine," she said. "I guess we can try one more time."

"Thank you," Tucker said. "You won't regret this." He held out the ticket. "On three, we both grab the ticket. Ready?"

Maya nodded.

"One, two," Tucker said, "three!"

Maya and Tucker each placed a hand on the ticket and closed their eyes.

Nothing happened, except that the storeroom door slammed open.

"What are you doing?!" Mom shrieked from the doorway. She ran over to them and grabbed the ticket out of their hands.

"Tucker, you know better than to disturb an artifact like this!" his mother shouted. She snatched the plastic sleeve from her son and carefully slipped the ticket back inside.

"We were being careful," Tucker protested. His face grew hot. He knew that he was blushing.

Tucker's mom quickly looked over the ticket. She took a deep breath and seemed to calm down once she realized the ticket was fine.

"I'm sorry for shouting," she said. "But if this had been ripped, or damaged in any way, it would lose all its magic."

Tucker and Maya looked at each other. Tucker knew what they were both thinking. The ticket had already lost its magic.

After Tucker's mom went over the Special Collection list they'd made, she put everything back inside the box. Then she ushered Maya and Tucker out of the storeroom. She took out a key and locked the door behind them. The deadbolt clicked loudly into place.

Tucker's shoulders sagged at the sound. *There goes our chance to save Liam and his parents*, he thought.

"I just can't understand why that box was labeled 'special,'" Tucker's mom said. She led the kids down the hall and back toward the museum's main gallery. Their footsteps echoed off the walls and the high ceiling.

"I mean, that violin was so damaged it was barely recognizable," she went on. "I have two better ones in the display case already."

"Yeah," Tucker agreed, glancing at Maya. "That stuff was junk."

Mom shook her head. "And I have full sets of

Titanic china in the exhibit already," she went on. "The ticket? I have a drawer full of them! And life vests in that condition are a dime a dozen."

"I guess all the survivors would have had one, huh?" Maya asked.

Mom nodded. "Most of them, yes," she said. She glanced at her watch. "I'm going to open the main gallery. You kids stay out of trouble — and out of the storeroom."

With a final glance at Maya and Tucker, Mom headed toward the front of the museum.

"Now what?" Maya asked.

"We have to get back," Tucker said. "We have to save him."

"But the storeroom is locked for the day," Maya said. "And besides, the ticket has lost its magic, just like your mom said."

"Maybe," Tucker said. "But that whole box was marked 'Special Collection.' Not just the ticket."

Maya's face brightened. "And like your mom

said, there was nothing special about any of those things," she said. "So . . . maybe that means . . ."

"There's nothing special that my mom knows about," Tucker added. "But you and I know better, right, Maya?"

Maya sighed. "We're going to play assistant curator again tomorrow morning, aren't we?" she asked.

Tucker nodded.

Maya shrugged. "This might turn out to be a pretty interesting spring break after all," she said. She and Tucker strolled across the front hall to watch the crowds as they came in.

RETURN TO
TITANIC

CONTINUES IN BOOK

1   2   3   4   .

STOWAWAYS

RETURN TO TITANIC

TIME VOYAGE

1

by STEVE BREZENOFF

RETURN TO TITANIC

STOWAWAYS

2

by STEVE BREZENOFF

RETURN TO TITANIC

AN UNSINKABLE SHIP

3

by STEVE BREZENOFF

RETURN TO TITANIC

OVERBOARD

4

by STEVE BREZENOFF

①

②

③

④

PASSENGER MANIFEST

While Tucker, Maya, and Liam are all fictional characters, the story of the *RMS Titanic* and its passengers is very real. In fact, some characters throughout the "Return to Titanic" series are based on real people.

1		**JOHN COFFEY** FIREMAN
2		**VIOLET JESSOP** STEWARDESS
3		**JOHN JACOB ASTOR IV** FIRST-CLASS PASSENGER
4		**EDWARD SMITH** CAPTAIN

John Coffey

JOHN COFFEY

John Coffey, a character featured in *Time Voyage*, was a real crewmember aboard the *Titanic* when it set sail on its maiden voyage. Coffey was a fireman, meaning his job was to shovel coal into *Titanic*'s massive furnaces and make sure it was properly spread. As a fireman, Coffey earned about six pounds a month.

Coffey really did jump ship in Queenstown, Ireland. He came ashore by stowing away on a tender and hiding among the mailbags. He later stated that he deserted his post aboard the *Titanic* because of a superstition he had about sailing, specifically about traveling on the *Titanic*. Three days after jumping ship, Coffey joined the crew of the *RMS Mauretania*. According to family lore, Coffey later claimed he'd left *Titanic* because he'd dreamed that the ship would sink. He lived to the age of 68.

HISTORICAL FILES

Construction of the *RMS Titanic* began in Belfast, Ireland on March 31, 1909. *Titanic* was built by Harland and Wolff, a ship-building company located in Belfast. The ocean liner was one of three ships commissioned by the White Star Line that were designated the "Olympic class" – ships that would cater to the most elite of passengers. The other two ships were the *Olympic* and the *Britannic*.

From the start, *Titanic* was designed to be the largest ship ever built. The White Star Line spared no expense when it came to constructing and outfitting the luxury ocean liner. When the final cost was tallied, it cost $7.5 million to build the *Titanic*. Today, it would cost approximately $400 million to build the same ship.

When complete, the *Titanic* was more than 882 feet long, weighed more than 46,000 tons, and was approximately 11 stories tall. *Titanic* was billed as "unsinkable" thanks to the 16 watertight compartments within the ship. Even if the first four compartments flooded, *Titanic* could stay afloat.

On April 10, 1912, *Titanic* set sail from Southampton, England on its maiden voyage with more than 2,200 people aboard. *Titanic* sailed first to Cherbourg, France and then to Queenstown, Ireland before setting off for its final destination, New York.

Altogether, it took three years for construction of the *Titanic* to be completed. It took only three hours for the entire ship to sink to the bottom of the Atlantic Ocean.

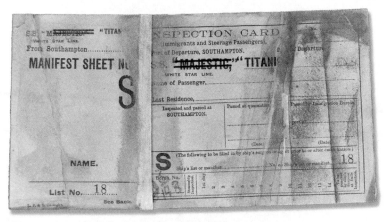

Steerage Inspection Card (boarding pass), 1912

AUTHOR

Steve Brezenoff lives in St. Paul, Minnesota, with his wife, Beth, their son, Sam, and their small, smelly dog, Harry. Besides writing books, he enjoys playing video games, riding his bicycle, and helping middle-school students to improve their writing skills. Steve's ideas almost always come to him in his dreams, so he does his best writing in his pajamas.

ILLUSTRATOR

At a young age, Scott Murphy filled countless sketchbooks with video game and comic book characters. After being convinced by his high school art teacher that he could make a living creating what he loves, Scott jumped headfirst into the artistic pool and hasn't come up for air since. He currently resides in New York City and loves every minute of it.